The Beginning of
the Armadillos

RUDYARD KIPLING

Illustrated by Lorinda Bryan Cauley

The Beginning of the Armadillos

HARCOURT BRACE & COMPANY

SAN DIEGO   NEW YORK   LONDON

Other picture books illustrated by Lorinda Bryan Cauley

THE UGLY DUCKLING
by Hans Christian Andersen

THE ELEPHANT'S CHILD
by Rudyard Kipling

GUNGA DIN
by Rudyard Kipling

THE GOODNIGHT CIRCLE
by Carolyn Lesser

PUSS IN BOOTS
by Charles Perrault

Written and illustrated by Lorinda Bryan Cauley

THE TROUBLE WITH TYRANNOSAURUS REX

Requests for permission to make copies of any part of the work should be mailed to:
Permissions Department,
Harcourt Brace & Company, 6277 Sea Harbor Drive,
Orlando, Florida 32887-6777.

LIBRARY OF CONGRESS CATALOGING-IN-PUBLICATION DATA
Kipling, Rudyard, 1865–1936.
The beginning of the armadillos.
Summary: A tortoise and a hedgehog combine their natural assets and transform
themselves into armadillos to escape the hungry attention of a young jaguar.
1. Children's stories, English. [1. Armadillos — Fiction.
2. Animals — Fiction. 3. Jungles — Fiction]
I. Cauley, Lorinda Bryan, ill. II. Title.
PZ7.K632Be   1985   [E]   85-5444
ISBN 0-15-206380-3
ISBN 0-15-206381-1 (pbk.)

Designed by Michael Farmer
Printed and bound by South China Printing Company, Hong Kong
B C D E F G
D E F G (pbk.)

Printed in Hong Kong

For Henry and Michelle
—L.B.C.

his, O Best Beloved, is another story of the High and Far-Off Times. In the very middle of those times was a Stickly-Prickly Hedgehog, and he lived on the banks of the turbid Amazon, eating shelly snails and things. And he had a friend, a Slow-and-Solid Tortoise, who lived on the banks of the turbid Amazon, eating green lettuces and things. And so *that* was all right, Best Beloved. Do you see?

But also, and at the same time, in those High and Far-Off Times, there was a Painted Jaguar, and he lived on the banks of the turbid Amazon too; and he ate everything that he could catch. When he could not catch deer or monkeys he would eat frogs and beetles; and when he could not catch frogs and beetles he went to his Mother Jaguar, and she told him how

to eat hedgehogs and tortoises.

She said to him ever so many times, graciously waving her tail, "My son, when you find a Hedgehog you must drop him into the water and then he will uncoil, and when you catch a Tortoise you must scoop him out of his shell with your paw." And so that was all right, Best Beloved.

One beautiful night on the banks of the turbid Amazon, Painted Jaguar found Stickly-Prickly Hedgehog and Slow-Solid Tortoise sitting under the trunk of a fallen tree. They could not run away, and so Stickly-Prickly Hedgehog curled himself up into a ball, because he was a Hedgehog, and Slow-Solid Tortoise drew in his head and feet into his shell as far as they would go, because he was a Tortoise; and so that was all right, Best Beloved. Do you see?

"Now attend to me," said Painted Jaguar, "because this is very important. My mother said that when I meet a Hedgehog I am to drop him into the water and then he will uncoil, and when I meet a Tortoise I am to scoop him out of his shell with my paw. Now which of you is Hedgehog, and which is Tortoise? because, to save my spots, I can't tell."

"Are you sure of what your Mummy told you?" said Stickly-Prickly Hedgehog. "Are you quite sure? Perhaps she said that when you uncoil a Tortoise you must shell him out of the water with a scoop, and when you paw a Hedgehog you must drop him on the shell."

"Are you sure of what your Mummy told you?" said Slow-and-Solid Tortoise. "Are you quite sure? Perhaps she said that when you water a Hedgehog you must drop him into your paw, and when you meet a Tortoise you must shell him till he uncoils."

"I don't think it was at all like that," said Painted Jaguar, but he felt a little puzzled; "but, please, say it again more distinctly."

"When you scoop water with your paw you uncoil it with a Hedgehog," said Stickly-Prickly. "Remember that, because it's important."

"*But,*" said the Tortoise, "when you paw your meat you drop it into a Tortoise with a scoop. Why can't you understand?"

"You are making my spots ache," said Painted Jaguar; "and besides, I didn't want your advice at all. I only wanted to know which of you is Hedgehog and which is Tortoise."

"I shan't tell you," said Stickly-Prickly, "but you can scoop me out of my shell if you like."

"Aha!" said Painted Jaguar. "Now I know you're Tortoise. You thought I wouldn't! Now I will." Painted Jaguar darted out his paddy-paw just as

Stickly-Prickly curled himself up, and of course Jaguar's paddy-paw
was just filled with prickles. Worse than that, he knocked Stickly-Prickly
away and away into the woods and the bushes, where it was too dark
to find him.

Then he put his paddy-paw into his mouth, and of course the prickles hurt him worse than ever. As soon as he could speak, he said, "Now I know he isn't Tortoise at all. But"—and then he scratched his head with his unprickly paw—"how do I know that this other is Tortoise?"

"But I *am* Tortoise," said Slow-and-Solid. "Your mother was quite right.

She said that you were to scoop me out of my shell with your paw. Begin."

"You didn't say she said that a minute ago," said Painted Jaguar, sucking the prickles out of his paddy-paw. "You said she said something quite different."

"Well, suppose you say that I said that she said something quite different, I don't see that it makes any difference; because if she said what you said I said she said, it's just the same as if I said what she said she said. On the other hand, if you think she said that you were to uncoil me with a scoop, instead of pawing me into drops with a shell, I can't help that, can I?"

"But you said you wanted to be scooped out of your shell with my paw," said Painted Jaguar.

"If you'll think again you'll find I didn't say anything of the kind. I said that your mother said that you were to scoop me out of my shell," said Slow-and-Solid.

"What will happen if I do?" said the Jaguar most sniffily and most cautious.
"I don't know, because I've never been scooped out of my shell before;
but I tell you truly, if you want to see me swim away you've only got to drop
me into the water."

"I don't believe it," said Painted Jaguar. "You've mixed up all the things my mother told me to do with the things that you asked me whether I was sure that she didn't say, till I don't know whether I'm on my head or my painted tail; and now you come and tell me something I *can* understand, and it makes me more mixy than before. My mother told me that I was to drop one of you into the water, and as you seem so anxious to be dropped I think you don't want to be dropped. So jump into the turbid Amazon and be quick about it."

"I warn you that your Mummy won't be pleased. Don't tell her I didn't tell you," said Slow-Solid.

"If you say another word about what my mother said—" the Jaguar answered, but he had not finished the sentence before Slow-and-Solid quietly dived into the turbid Amazon, swam under water for a long way, and came out on the bank where Stickly-Prickly was waiting for him.

"That was a very narrow escape," said Stickly-Prickly. "I don't like Painted Jaguar. What did you tell him that you were?"

"I told him truthfully that I was a truthful Tortoise, but he wouldn't believe it, and he made me jump into the river to see if I was, and I was, and he is surprised. Now he's gone to tell his Mummy. Listen to him!"

They could hear Painted Jaguar roaring up and down among the trees and the bushes by the side of the turbid Amazon, till his Mummy came.

"Son, son!" said his mother ever so many times, graciously waving her tail, "what have you been doing that you shouldn't have done?"

"I tried to scoop something that said it wanted to be scooped out of its shell with my paw, and my paw is full of per-ickles," said Painted Jaguar.

"Son, son!" said his mother ever so many times, graciously waving her tail, "by the prickles in your paddy-paw I see that that must have been a Hedgehog. You should have dropped him into the water."

"I did that to the other thing; and he said he was a Tortoise, and I didn't believe him, and it was quite true, and he has dived under the turbid Amazon, and he won't come up again, and I haven't anything at all to eat, and I think we had better find lodgings somewhere else. They are too clever on the turbid Amazon for poor me!"

"Son, son!" said his mother ever so many times, graciously waving her tail, "now attend to me and remember what I say. A Hedgehog curls himself up into a ball and his prickles stick out every which way at once. By this you may know the Hedgehog."

"I don't like this old lady one little bit," said Stickly-Prickly, under the shadow of a large leaf. "I wonder what else she knows?"

"A Tortoise can't curl himself up," Mother Jaguar went on, ever so many times, graciously waving her tail. "He only draws his head and legs into his shell. By this way you may know the Tortoise."

"I don't like this old lady at all—at all," said Slow-and-Solid Tortoise. "Even Painted Jaguar can't forget those directions. It's a great pity that you can't swim, Stickly-Prickly."

"Don't talk to me," said Stickly-Prickly. "Just think how much better it would be if you could curl up. This *is* a mess! Listen to Painted Jaguar."

Painted Jaguar was sitting on the banks of the turbid Amazon sucking prickles out of his paws and saying to himself—

"*Can't curl, but can swim—*
Slow-Solid, that's him!
Curls up, but can't swim—
Stickly-Prickly, that's him!"

"He'll never forget that this month of Sundays," said Stickly-Prickly. "Hold up my chin, Slow-and-Solid. I'm going to try to learn to swim. It may be useful."

"Excellent!" said Slow-and-Solid; and he held Stickly-Prickly's chin, while Stickly-Prickly kicked in the waters of the turbid Amazon.

"You'll make a fine swimmer yet," said Slow-and-Solid. "Now, if you can unlace my back plates a little, I'll see what I can do toward curling up. It may be useful."

Stickly-Prickly helped to unlace Tortoise's back plates, so that by twisting and straining Slow-and-Solid actually managed to curl up a tiddy wee bit.

"Excellent!" said Stickly-Prickly; "but I shouldn't do any more just now. It's making you black in the face. Kindly lead me into the water once again and I'll practice that sidestroke which you say is so easy." And so Stickly-Prickly practiced, and Slow-Solid swam alongside.

"Excellent!" said Slow-and-Solid. "A little more practice will make you a regular whale. Now, if I may trouble you to unlace my back and front plates two holes more, I'll try that fascinating bend that you say is so easy. Won't Painted Jaguar be surprised!"

"Excellent!" said Stickly-Prickly, all wet from the turbid Amazon. "I declare, I shouldn't know you from one of my own family. Two holes, I think, you said? A little more expression, please, and don't grunt quite so much, or Painted Jaguar may hear us. When you've finished, I want to try that long dive which you say is so easy. Won't Painted Jaguar be surprised!"

And so Stickly-Prickly dived, and Slow-and-Solid dived alongside.

"Excellent!" said Slow-and-Solid. "A leetle more attention to holding your breath and you will be able to keep house at the bottom of the turbid Amazon. Now I'll try that exercise of wrapping my hind legs round my ears which you say is so peculiarly comfortable. Won't Painted Jaguar be surprised!"

"Excellent!" said Stickly-Prickly. "But it's straining your back plates a little. They are all overlapping now, instead of lying side by side."

"Oh, that's the result of exercise," said Slow-and-Solid. "I've noticed that your prickles seem to be melting into one another, and that you're growing to look rather more like a pinecone, and less like a chestnut burr, than you used to."

"Am I?" said Stickly-Prickly. "That comes from my soaking in the water. Oh, won't Painted Jaguar be surprised!"

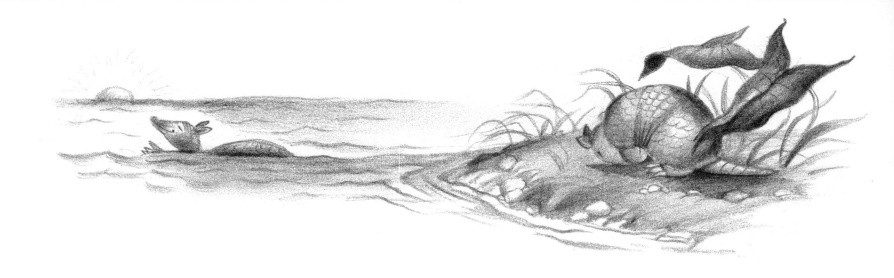

They went on with their exercises, each helping the other, till
morning came; and when the sun was high they rested and dried
themselves. Then they saw that they were both of them quite different
from what they had been.

"Stickly-Prickly," said Tortoise after breakfast, "I am not what I was yesterday; but I think that I may yet amuse Painted Jaguar."

"That was the very thing I was thinking just now," said Stickly-Prickly. "I think scales are a tremendous improvement on prickles—to say nothing of being able to swim. Oh, *won't* Painted Jaguar be surprised! Let's go and find him."

By and by they found Painted Jaguar, still nursing his paddy-paw that had been hurt the night before. He was so astonished that he fell three times backward over his own painted tail without stopping.

"Good morning!" said Stickly-Prickly. "And how is your dear gracious Mummy this morning?"

"She is quite well, thank you," said Painted Jaguar; "but you must forgive me if I do not at this precise moment recall your name."

"That's unkind of you," said Stickly-Prickly, "seeing that this time yesterday you tried to scoop me out of my shell with your paw."

"But you hadn't any shell. It was all prickles," said Painted Jaguar. "I know it was. Just look at my paw!"

"You told me to drop into the turbid Amazon and be drowned," said Slow-Solid. "Why are you so rude and forgetful today?"

"Don't you remember what your mother told you?" said Stickly-Prickly—

> "Can't curl, but can swim—
> Stickly-Prickly, that's him!
> Curls up, but can't swim—
> Slow-Solid, that's him!"

Then they both curled themselves up and rolled round and round Painted Jaguar till his eyes turned truly cartwheels in his head.

Then he went to fetch his mother.

"Mother," he said, "there are two new animals in the woods today, and the one that you said couldn't swim, swims, and the one that you said couldn't curl up, curls; and they've gone shares in their prickles, I think, because both of them are scaly all over, instead of one being smooth and the other prickly; and, besides that, they are rolling round and round in circles, and I don't feel comfy."

"Son, son!" said Mother Jaguar ever so many times, graciously waving
her tail, "a Hedgehog is a Hedgehog, and can't be anything but a Hedgehog;
and a Tortoise is a Tortoise, and can never be anything else."

"But it isn't a Hedgehog, and it isn't a Tortoise. It's a little of both, and I
don't know its proper name."

"Nonsense!" said Mother Jaguar. "Everything has its proper name. I
should call it 'Armadillo' till I found out the real one. And I should leave
it alone."

So *that's* all right, Best Beloved. Do you see?

So Painted Jaguar did as he was told, especially about leaving them alone; but the curious thing is that from that day to this, O Best Beloved, no one on the banks of the turbid Amazon has ever called Stickly-Prickly and Slow-Solid anything except Armadillo. There are Hedgehogs and Tortoises in other places, of course (there are some in my garden); but the real old and clever kind, with their scales lying lippety-lappety one over the other, like pinecone scales, that lived on the banks of the turbid Amazon in the High and Far-Off Days, are always called Armadillos, because they were so clever.